I0572307

RUDY
PROJECT
Bapco
energies
RUDY
PROJECT
MERIDA

INEOS
WORLD TOUR
73
UCI
MOST
MOST
PINARELLO
C60
C60
Continental
GRAND PRIX 5000
GRAND PRIX 5000

MOMENTS OF PRO

Professional cycling. A captivating colourful blur of skill and power, performed by incredible athletes.

Once you start to gain an understanding of the stages, strategy, lingo and Lycra, you have a lot of late nights to look forward too. You aren't turning off that TV once the breakaway looks to be a chance of success.

Even my own mum succumbed to the famous yellow jersey every July. Originally, she liked the colours the riders wore, and admiring castles and villages. It didn't take too many editions before she was questioning the reckless decision making behind a futile breakaway attempt or airing her distaste for an overzealous sicky bottle incident.

If you can get to a few races, you will soon see that professional cycling is a great live spectacle for any sports fan. Speed and skill must combine seamlessly with science and strategy; it's a captivating atmosphere. Not everyone needs to be snapping hundreds of photos, but there are some of us who do.

The many moving parts to professional cycling have always fascinated me. I created this photo journal with the pro team mechanics, soigneurs and helpers in mind. Then comes the race infrastructure and media which brings it all together for us all to enjoy.

The images featured are a collection from the many races I have managed to attend in Australia, including my annual pilgrimage to Adelaide for the Tour down Under.

These are all my own images. From rider preparation to team celebration, my aim was to capture a bit of everything that brings professional cycling to life.

A Ride Iconic project created by Shane Ellis, this is Moments of pro. Professional cycling captured through the lens of an avid enthusiast.

174
172
173

LAB71
vittoria CORSA PRO
vittoria CORSA PRO
Vision
Vision
Vision
60 SL
vittoria

CANYON
AEROAD
AEROAD
CANYON
CANYON
CANYON
CUSTOMRACEPLUS
ZIPP
XS
SRAM

JULIAN
ALAPHILIPPE

V·A·M
CLARKE
Simon
OSTRO
FACTOR

Sagan
BORA
hansgrohe

VISION
45 SL
vittoria
MUC-OFF
VERSITY
RALIA

CORSA PRO
EASTON
60s

Groupama
FDJ
FDJ
CYCLISTE
Wilier

CHARGED
ON-SPORTS.COM
3.0ᵃʰ

Marek
BAJFUS
30.
Qilive

CARBON-TI
CARBON-TI
CARBON-TI
55-40 EVO

Vision
cannondale
cannondale

WATTS
NO GLORY
MOMODES

OFF
Mu
MUC-OFF·Off
-OFF
JE
NT
ER
MUC-OFF
EF Education
PROTOTYPE
TACKY 3
-Off
CANT
US FL.OZ
Bike Society Adelaide
Muc-Off MO-94 400ml Aerosol
$11.95
sinter
Santos
tour
down
under
9

ÖTZ
TAL
BORA
sgrohe
Red Bull
BOSS
grenke
TEAM
RedBull
BOR
S-WORKS

Santini
ADELAIDE
SOUTH AUSTRALIA
Red Bull
BORA
hansgrohe
genke
BOSS
mewa
ÖTZ
TAL
Ziptrak
BORA
hansgrohe
81
81
UCI WORLD TOUR
UCI WORLD TOUR

BREEZY ON BY
Z1
LAZER Z1
KEEP COOL
WELCOME TO SUMMER
LAZER
LAZER
Sophia SAMMONS
Z1
G'DAY
LAZER
RACE THE BRUTE LAZER

GOBIK
FDJ
SUEZ
futuroscope
SOFIBRIE
GRAND POITIERS
Communauté urbaine
Vienne
Nouvelle-Aquitaine
36
FDJ
SUEZ
GOBIK

AE
Emirates
UAE

ALULA
CADEX
RUBY
ayco
LIV
DURA-ACE
CADEX

RUDY
UCI WORLD TOUR
SOUDAL
RIDLEY
G&V
ENERGY GROUP
vermarc
GAERNE
lotto
UCI WORLD TOUR
BONTRAGER
TREK

100%

Cofidis
Nalini
Cofidis
Nalini
KR1

BÂR CLIF
cervélo
ROT
BIKE·COMP
CAS

COMMISSAIRE
UCI

Mitchelton
Bay Cycling Classic
BUDGET
FORKLIFTS
BUDGET
FORKLIFTS
Chain Reaction
Cycles.com

EFN - MEN'S STAGE 3
NORWOOD - URAIDLA

Santos
HEALTH PARTNERS - M
NDA - TANUNDA
UAE TEAM
EMIRATES XRG
SOUDAL
QUICK STEP
TREK
UCI WORLD TEAM
Santini
PIRELLI
SRAM

BE - MEN'S STAGE 6
DE - ADELAIDE
SCHWALBE
AE TEAM
RATES XRG
SOUDAL
QUICK-STEP
DECATHLON AG2R
LA MONDIALE TEAM
INTERMARCHÉ -
WANTY
INEOS GRENADIERS
HA
41
42
43
44
45
46
47
51
52
53
54
55
56
57
61
62
63
64
65
66
67
71
72
73
74
75
76
77
81
82
83
84
85
86
87
Magnus
EF EDUCATION -
EASYPOST
ALPECIN-
DECEUNINC
LIDL-TREK
GROUPAMA-
171
172
173
181
182
183

Km | Location | Food
10 | GPM 2
30
39 | Sprint
50
60
70
80
90
100
106 | GPM 1
112 | Sprint
130
141 | GPM 1
147 | FINISH
Boven

EF / PRO CYCLING
easypost
THE ORIGINAL
OATLY
AMACX
aevolo
cannondale

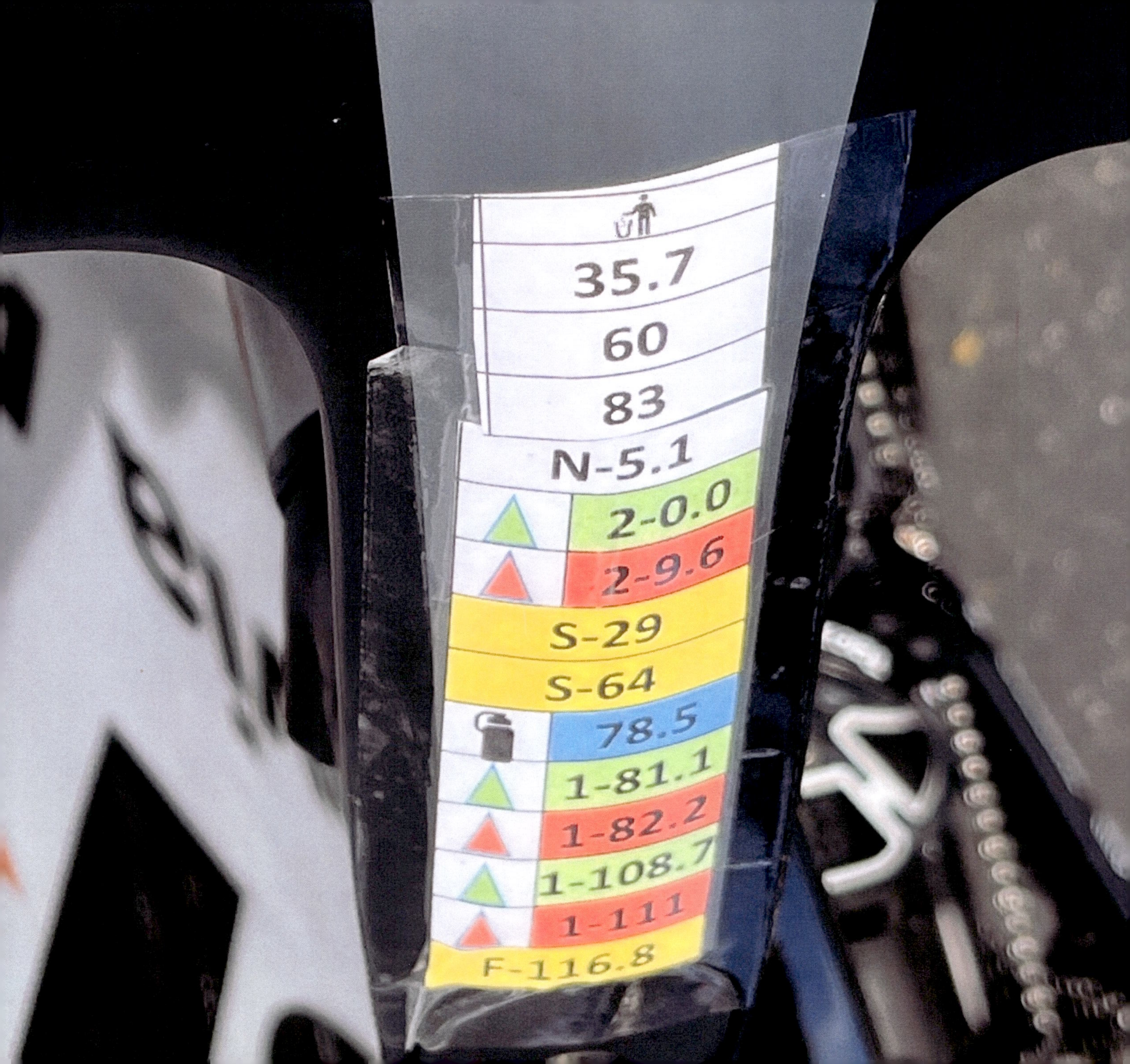
35.7
60
83
N-5.1
2-0.0
2-9.6
S-29
S-64
78.5
1-81.1
1-82.2
1-108.7
1-111
F-116.8

BORA
BRIGHT
WIPE
ANTIFOG
20

NT PARKING
STRICTIONS
CHWALBE
PLICABLE
SCHWALBE 100
SCHWALBE
SCHWALBE 150
SCHWALBE 200
GARMIN
CITY OF ADELAIDE

Santos
UAE Emirates
Santos
OFFICIAL CREW

LIDL
LIDL

Santos
ADELAIDE
Santos
THINK! ROAD SAFETY STAGE 5
2:25:16
GARM
ARKEA
SAMSIC
BAHRAIN
VICTORIOUS
BORA

lease
a bike
AMACX
GARMIN
lease
a bike
AMACX
SPORTS NUTRITION
beyond
victory
JUMBO

MADAM
ARIAN
ms
SUMMER
of CYCL
VICTORIA
lotto

King of
Mountain

LEGEND

Ride Iconic.

A Ride Iconic project. All things bike related, captured through the lens of an avid enthusiast.

Project: Moments of pro.
Location: Adelaide and Melbourne Australia
Creator and photographer: Shane Ellis, Melbourne Australia.
Camera: Canon 600D, Apple iPhone (various)
Images taken: 2016 - 2025
Instagram: rideiconic
Web: www.rideiconic.com
Contact: info@rideiconic.com

With thanks: Thank you to the Tour Down Under, for the incredible access they make available to fans and enthusiasts of professional cycling.